T0130414

AQUILLO
COMICS

ISSUE #3

JURASSIC SENTRIES

" REMATCH "

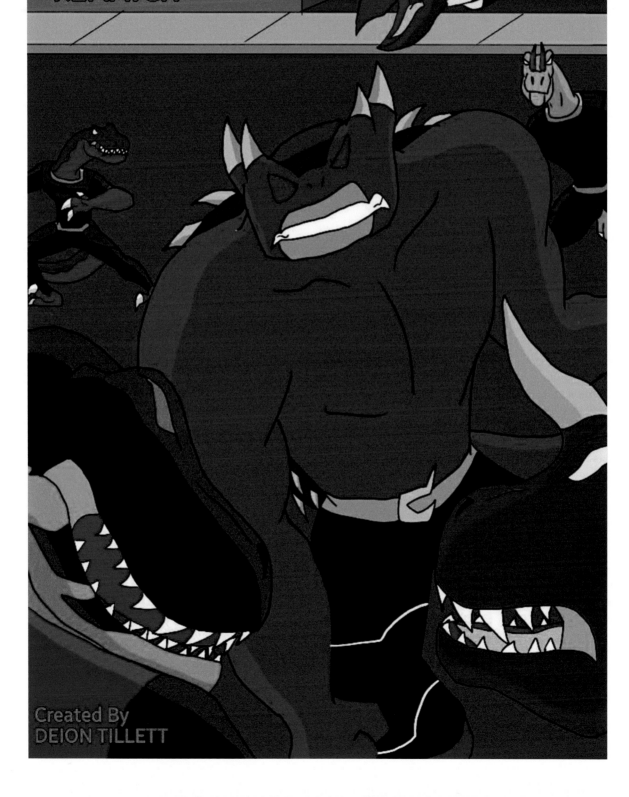

Created By
DEION TILLETT

Copyright © 2021 by Deion Tillett. 836123

All rights reserved. No part of this book may
be reproduced or transmitted in any form or by
any means, electronic or mechanical, including
photocopying, recording, or by any information storage
and retrieval system, without permission in writing from
the copyright owner.

This is a work of fiction. Names, characters,
places and incidents either are the product of the
author's imagination or are used fictitiously, and any
resemblance to any actual persons, living or dead,
events, or locales is entirely coincidental.

To order additional copies of this book, contact:
Xlibris
844-714-8691
www.Xlibris.com
Orders@Xlibris.com

ISBN: Softcover   978-1-6641-9633-9
         EBook   978-1-6641-9634-6

Print information available on the last page

Rev. date: 10/22/2021

PREVIOUSLY ON

JURASSIC SENTRIES

When the Cretaceous Conquers arrive to Earth after fifteen years, the young Sentries prepared for battle. During the fight on the ground with four of Spinus' elite warriors, Rex frees the captured Sentries on the Conquers warship.

The Sentries cripple the warship, causing the Conquers to fallback.

Now with the city saved, their secret is out and they must face whatever obstacle approaches them next.

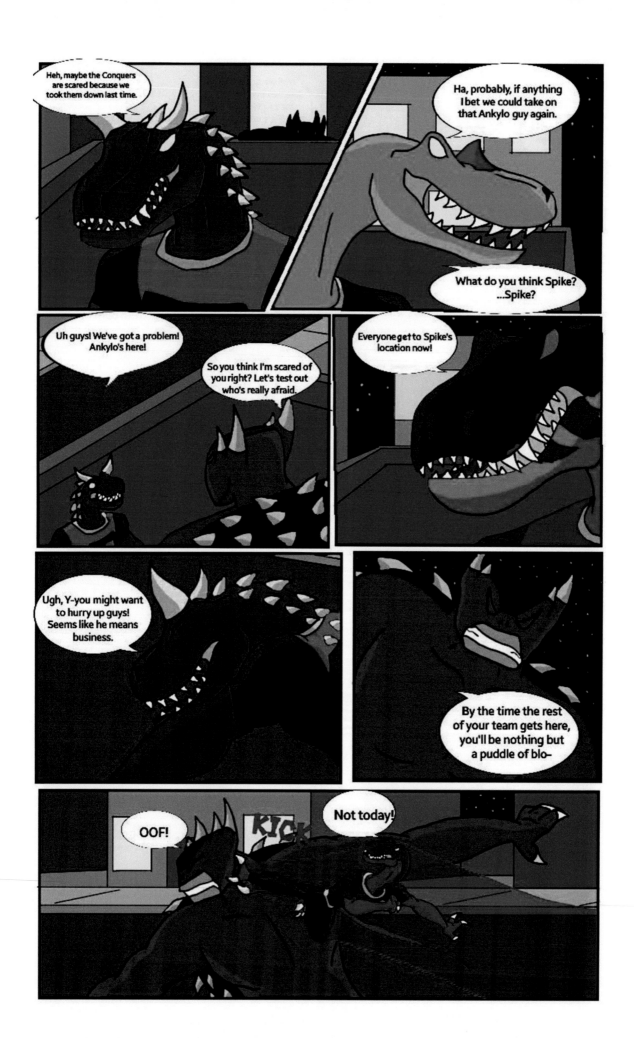

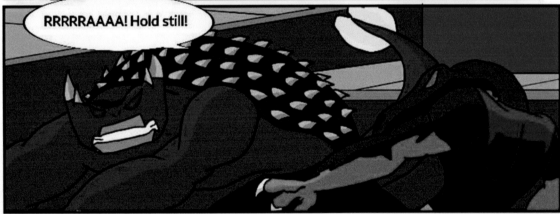

JURASSIC SENTRIES

ISSUE #4

NEXT ISSUE : " DR. KORROSAVE "

Created By
DEION TILLETT

Printed in the United States
by Baker & Taylor Publisher Services